TWEETY

Plays *Catch*
the
Puddy Tat

by Eileen Daly

illustrated by Peter Alvarado and William Lorencz

A GOLDEN BOOK • NEW YORK

Western Publishing Company, Inc.

Racine, Wisconsin 53404

I think I'd better find that puddy tat, Tweety decided.
*He's always twying to catch me, so I'm safer if I know
where he is!* He flew down to the floor, hoping to see
Sylvester curled up in his favorite snoozing place.

But Sylvester was in the kitchen, and he seemed
very busy. Tweety peeked around the corner.

"I wonder what the puddy tat is baking," said Tweety to himself. "It smells vewy tasty."

Then he heard Sylvester call, "Tweety! Tweety Bird! I've got a present for you."

Oh, goody! thought Tweety. *The puddy tat wants to be fwiends again.* He flew into the kitchen. "What's my pwesent?" he asked.

"Birdseed flapjacks," said Sylvester, "made just for you." He flipped one quickly into the air, and it fell —*plop!*—right on Tweety.

"O-o-oh!" cried Tweety. "My fwapjack is *too big!*"

"Not for me," said Sylvester. "It's just right, with a Tweety Bird inside." He pounced, but the flapjack —and Tweety—disappeared under the stove.

"That was a naughty puddy tat," said Tweety. "I would wike to be fwiends with you, but you make it so hard."

"No harm meant, Tweety," said Sylvester. "I just like to play Catch the Tweety Bird."

"Let's pway Catch the Puddy Tat for a wittle while," suggested Tweety, but Sylvester just yawned and fell asleep.

Tweety escaped from under the stove and flew up to the attic.

"I weally do need a west fwom that puddy tat," he said as he perched on a birdcage. "But how can I make him stop chasing me?"

Then Tweety looked into the cage and had an idea. He searched the attic and finally found just what he wanted—a paper bird hanging from a string.

Tweety put the paper bird far back inside the cage. "Puddy Tat will think the bird is a weal one. He will have to go inside to get it—and I will twap him in the birdcage."

Tweety hid beside the open birdcage door. Then he began to sing.

Soon he heard Sylvester call, "Tweety? Did I hear you up here?"

Suddenly Sylvester spied the cage and, inside, what he thought was a bird. "Aha!" he exclaimed and pounced into the open cage.

Tweety slammed the door shut. "Aha yourself!" he said. "Now you can't get out, and I will have a west."

"A rest, eh?" said Sylvester after a minute. "Well, keep your eyes open, Tweety. I think you are about to see a cage walking."

Sylvester put his legs through the wires and walked away to find a wire cutter.

Soon he had cut his way out and was again chasing poor Tweety.

"Puddy Tat," Tweety puffed, out of breath, "I am getting so vewy sweepy. I wish you would go away for a wong time."

Later Tweety asked himself, "What *would* make him go away? Something scawy, maybe. . . ."

While Sylvester was sleeping, Tweety thought and thought. *That puddy tat is pwetty bwave,* recalled Tweety. *It will take something* **weally** *scawy to fwighten him away.*

"I know," he said. "I'll be a witch—a scawy witch. That should make the puddy tat go away for a w-o-o-ong time."

Tweety made himself look like a scary witch. He flew over Sylvester's head. *Swish!*

"W*oooo-oo-OOO!*" said the Tweety-witch.

Sylvester opened one eye. Then he opened the other. "Wh-what was *that?*" he asked, standing up and looking around.

"A witch," said the Tweety-witch.

"A witch, eh?" said Sylvester. "You're a very small witch, aren't you?"

"Well, yes," said the Tweety-witch. "But you know what small witches do, don't you?"

"What?" asked Sylvester, backing away just a little bit.

"We cast spells—*bad* ones. We can change cats into tiny mice."

"Into m-mice! Can you—uh—*really* do that?" asked Sylvester, backing away a little faster.

"It's my favowite spell," said the Tweety-witch. "I'll show you." He began to wave his broom.

"No! Don't!" shouted Sylvester, and he ran out the door and through the gate.

"I'm starting the spell," said the Tweety-witch as he flew just above Sylvester's ear. "One, two, *ka-zip, ka-zip*. . . ."

Sylvester ran faster—so fast that he didn't see where he was going.

"Wook out!" shouted Tweety, but it was too late. Sylvester was right at the edge of a pond. He couldn't stop, so he took a mighty leap and landed beside a big rock. After a minute, he climbed up on the rock. He looked back and saw Tweety, who had taken off his witch mask.

"Tweety!" exclaimed Sylvester. Then he said, "I —uh—knew that was you all the time."

"Are you all wight, Puddy Tat?" Tweety called.

"No!" said Sylvester. "Cats don't like water. Help me!" Sylvester pointed to the shore. "Sail that little boat over and rescue me."

But Tweety wouldn't do it. "You were a naughty puddy tat," he said, and he flew home, leaving Sylvester marooned.

For a little while, Tweety was happy all by himself. Then a strange thing happened. He grew lonesome. "I never thought I'd miss that pesky puddy tat," he said to himself. "I even miss being chased!"

Finally he flew back to see how Sylvester was getting along. And what did Tweety find? Sylvester was even more lonesome than Tweety!

"Poor Puddy Tat," said Tweety. "If I wescue you, will you pwomise not to pway chase *all* the time?"

"I promise, I promise," said Sylvester.

So Tweety sailed the little boat over to the rock, and Sylvester sailed it back.

And the next day, Sylvester chased Tweety only twice—once before breakfast and once before dinner.